BEING A WIFE

To Tari
Descover your Joy
Love
Linda

BEING A WIFE

LIVING THE LIFE OF A WIFE

LEOLA IRENE

To order additional copies of this book, contact:
Xlibris Corporation
1-888-795-4274
www.Xlibris.com
Orders@Xlibris.com
47442

CONTENTS

Thanks

Thank you God, I am so grateful for all that you are.

To My husband Darrell, who is my greatest gift from God. Thank you for all your encouragement, love and your strong supportive arms that hold me together.

To my daughter Aisha, you are such a blessing. Thank you for being there. The wisdom you hold is well beyond your years.

To my son Marwan, Thank you for all the words of encouragement and the love you give so freely.

Thank you to all my sisters that are a never-ending source of love, Kimberly Haynes, Alesia Dowden, Angela Fuller and Keesha Fuller.

To my Mom and Dad, Thank you for being a great example that love conquers all.

Thank you Tina Pullum for your poem "The Beauty of a Rose"

To Atherine "Ace" Blanco, Thank you so very much for being a great friend and for the genuine generosity of your gift.

Introduction

You have got to be a wife to live the life of a wife. Living the life of a wife has many challenges. Being a wife for over thirty years has taught me many lessons, ones—I wished I could have learned as a young girl. To know what was expected of me when I became a wife. As a young girl you are told about the knight in shinning armor, or the handsome prince. You are told about the husband you will marry someday, but they forgot to tell you what you are supposed to do with him once you are together. How do we live happily ever after, or does happily ever after truly exist.

This book is written with my beliefs of the Father, the Son and the Holy Spirit. I do acknowledge that you may not be a believer. If you are another faith or have no faith at all, this book is designed to help you. Many of the stories are life lessons. Life lessons that would have helped in our marriages a long time ago if only we had known. Some marriages might have been saved.

Now is the time to know about another way of seeing your life of a wife. You may be single and reading to get knowledge before the husband arrives or you may be a bride to be. Read and learn what things people may not have expressed or explained to you in your life's journey.

Seeing through my eyes, see the plant that creates the most beautiful flower in the world . . . The Rose. In the winter months when you purchase a rose plant, it came to you with bare roots. When you plant it into the ground; it has no leaves, just bare sticks that shoot out of the soil. The top or above the ground you cannot see the beauty. Below the roots are taking in all the nourishment they can hold then they grow outward and become strong.

In due season, which is its perfect time, the plant begins to sprout new beautiful stems. Then the leaves begin to appear, you look at the plant in a day or two and you can finally see a bud appearing. It is growing larger by the day and you cannot quite see the color or the flower it holds near. Then one day as the breeze blows and the sun glows the plant burst open to the glory of the flower. Each stem has a different flower just as beautiful as the next. All the flowers are beautiful, yet all different. Every pedal is soft, silky and vibrant, showing off its color that captivates your eyes. The rose's color draws you closer to smell the sweet fragrance that consumes its very presence. All that it is leaves and imprint with all your senses that you will remember forever.

My hopes are that this book will be to your life as the plant is to the rose. I hope that you will become stronger, able to withstand the test of time and when it is your time to bring fourth the beauty of the rose-The first rose will bring you love, the second rose will bring you joy, and another peace, and another patience, another kindness, another gentleness, another rose will bring you self-control and another faithfulness and another will bring you thankfulness. Know that the beauty of a rose is you.

Acknowledgements

In our journey of life, we meet people that are essential to who and what we are to become. These people are significant and of great value to my soul.

My Pastors, Bishop Edwin J. and Venita M. Derensbourg III, you continually point the way to God and are carriers of the truth. I am so grateful for you. Thank you

To all the other people that were divinely destined to cross my path in life's journey. Thank you for your love, prayers and the many words of encouragement. They are the following: Dawn Willis, Demetris Sewell, Addie Peters, Regina Murphy, LaTanya Freeman, Gwendolyn Derby, Barbara McNairy and Rosalind Bullock.

Prologue

There is a myriad of things that come together for the purpose of preparing you to become a bride.

In the beginning, there is a ring. Meticulous consideration for the diamond cut, color, clarity, and carat weight are of great concern. Many are with sparkling diamonds or some with other jewel that catch the attention—the eye—and are looked upon as a signal of love. The light's reflection on the jewels twinkles like the stars in the night's sky.

Then there is the engagement party where family and friends gather together to celebrate the bride—and groom-to-be. The planning of the engagement party can be as elaborate or as simple as can be, but there is still planning to be done. People come from miles around to enjoy the engagement party where there are gifts, plenty of food, drinks, and clever conversation. A toast to the bride—and groom-to-be, showing everyone's in agreement that these two are made for each other. Oh, and did I mention the gifts?

As we move into preparing to be a bride, finding the perfect place to hold the ceremony is the first decision the bride actually makes, besides saying yes to the proposal from the man she loves, of course. With this in mind, the place has to accommodate the number of guest that you have decided to invite. Is it a place where you can have the wedding and reception altogether? If there is no room for the reception, you must find a place to hold your guests with all the accommodations you choose to provide. The facilities usually spark the imagination of the bride on what her absolutely perfect wedding day will be.

There are the wedding planners—people that plan the entire wedding from start to finish.

Let's not fail to mention that there are books and systems online that can help plan your dream wedding. This information tells you, the bride, all the things needed and the proper etiquette that applies to every situation you may encounter. The planners give you time lines and dates that are your deadlines in sticking to the plan prepared for you. Now the real work begins, and remember, brides can and will change their minds throughout this preparation process.

There is the wedding decoration designer. This person designs the decorations for the ceremony, reception, and the bride and groom's brunch or send-off to the honeymoon celebration. The décor is coordinated to the bride's imagination where whatever will be, will be—lighting, flower arrangements, swags, centerpieces, cake decorations, coordinating colors, and fabrics are all to the pleasure of the bride-to-be.

The cake designer prepares the cake according to the specifications of the bride-to-be and has to have many different cake designs. Some designs have fountains, bridges, some flowers, some candles, and some have special lighting within the design. The lights can flash, run, blink, or just stay on to light up the cakes. Cakes can be the traditional three layers to seven or more in designs you could only imagine. Cakes have different flavors and colors and, of course, there is the icing in different flavors and colors; last but not least, the filling of the cake comes in different flavors as well. The cake can be sugar free. There is a cake tasting to see if the cake is moist and flavorful. The flavors are from traditional vanilla, chocolate, and strawberry to piña colada, mango, kiwi, fresh fruit, and/or jelly filling and so much more. The cake or cakes are set up into a special design to add a special pizzazz in the celebration of marriage for the bride and groom.

The catering is another part of the plan for the wedding. The caterers help the bride create a menu for the guests. They discuss dishes, stemware, silverware, and serving options. The caterers will give you the best time to serve and how it is to be served; what to serve to the children. They also plan the appetizers and drinks that are to be served (while the guests wait for the arrival of the bride and groom) and the drinks to be served during dinner and for the champagne toast. The caterers will prepare the food and drinks for the brunch or send-off celebration. There is a food tasting to see if you enjoy the flavor of the seasonings and the texture of the tender morsels, making sure that the food is prepared with the highest of standards, for this can also be another gathering of family and friends.

Let me remind you that we are talking about all the people and things that come together to support you in being a bride.

Music for the special event is a must. Will there be a live band or a DJ? Special songs are chosen for each part of the wedding—before, during the wedding, and reception.

You have a bartender that is on duty throughout the festivities, serving drinks to the guests to make them feel comfortable.

Invitations are designed by graphic artists or companies that can really put some details into invitations. Invitations can come with the traditional date and time, but now also there can be directions to the wedding and things to do while your guests are in town, the menu choices of what you would like to eat, and an RSVP card. The graphic designers also create the thank-you cards that complement the invitations and menus.

Capturing all the moments of the wedding day are your photographers and video people so you can look back and remember all the special events of the day, knowing that this is a time filled with love, laughter, and joys that life can bring.

The florist delivers and arranges the flowers that you have selected according to the special colors of the wedding and reception. Flowers are selected for the bride and the bridesmaids, the groom and the groomsmen, the parents and the grandparents. All are color coordinated and are selected by the bride for the wedding extravaganza.

You choose the bridal gown and the bridesmaids' dresses, the tuxedos for the groom and the groomsmen along with the fathers.

There are hostesses and/or ushers to help make the day flow smoother. A limousine service is chosen to whisk away the bride and groom.

Friends and family gather again to give the bridal shower where everyone showers the bride with love, gifts, and people giving their time to show how much they care.

Bridal registries are everywhere. Most retail stores have one. Now there are registries for the honeymoon. The Web sites will give you a virtual tour of the facility you have chosen. At the click of a button, you can purchase tours, candlelight dinners, dinner cruises, massage for two, scuba lessons or diving, golf, spa services, breakfast in bed, and many other services that are provided by this honeymoon service.

There are personal registries for clothing for the honeymoon. From formal wear to swim wear—like bikinis—the choice is yours. There are also registries for the bridal showers only or for lingerie of choice—there is something for everyone.

All the things that I have mentioned, and there are still things that I have missed, all fit together in preparation to become a bride. There is a team of overwhelming support from everyone. Once it is all said and done, all eyes await the moment the bride comes down the aisle to meet the groom, the love of her life, to engage in a ceremony that will transform her from a bride into a wife.

As you return home from the honeymoon, what preparations are carried out to help you live the life of a wife?

Imagine with me for a moment. At the end of the honeymoon as you arrive at the airport for your departure. You are checking your bags in for the trip home. You look around, and all around you are bags—large bags, small bags of different shapes, models, and colors. All the tags have your name on them. The sign says that you can only take with you three bags, but you have all these bags that you cannot take with you.

It is time to make some decisions.

Looking through the bags, you choose what to take with you and what you must leave behind. You unpack and leave behind disappointments, hurts and pains. You are breaking away from old patterns of thinking. Then you reflect on; the marriage relationships of your family, your mother, your grandmother, aunts and cousins. What parts will you choose to take with you? What parts will you choose to leave behind? Contemplating within yourself; can you surrender to love him as you love yourself? When you choose to marry, you are choosing to take on a new lifestyle. You are going to a new destination, one that you have chosen with great expectation. Even though you are looking forward, I would like you to look a bit farther ahead because there is another way to live the life of a wife.

Part 1

SURRENDERING TO LOVE

Love is something many people desire. Many people feel that they are in love, but do not seem to feel loved themselves. I believe that finding true love is a yearning that lives in the heart of man. When I say true love, it means love with the truth of God's word.

The Bible says in Ephesians 5:22-33

Wives submit to your own husbands, as to the Lord. For the husband is the head of the wife, as also Christ is the head of the Church, and He is the Savior of the body. Therefore, just as the church is subject to Christ, so let the wives be to their own husbands in everything.

Husbands, love your wives just as Christ also loved the church and gave himself for her, that he might sanctify and cleanse her with the washing of the water by the word, that he might present her to himself a glorious church, not having spot or wrinkle or any such thing, but that she should be holy and without blemish.

So husbands ought to love their own wives as their own bodies; he who loves his wife loves himself. For no one ever hated his own flesh, but nourishes and cherishes it, just as the Lord does the church. For we are members of his body, of his flesh and of his bones.

For this reason, a man shall leave his father and mother and be joined to his wife, and the two shall become one flesh. This is a great mystery, but I speak concerning Christ and the church. Nevertheless, let each one of you in particular so love his own wife as himself, and let the wife see that she respects her husband. (NKJV)

The Bible says that the husband is the head of the wife. This puts the husband in a position of head of the household. Whatever his earning potential may be, he is still considered the head of the household. Even if he is a stay-at-home dad, or earns far less than the wife, he is still head of the household. When he is not walking in the fullness of God, he is still head of the household.

A husband would give his life; he protects, serves, teaches, and provides for his wife. Why, because of the love he ought to have for her. The husband is told to love his wife more than once. For the husband, one of the most important things in a marriage is to give love to his wife.

If you think about it for a moment, a woman with all the feelings and emotions she carries into the marriage, it is crucial to the relationship, between the two of them that love would be a continuous flow from the husband. This could be a reason why a marriage where the man loves the woman more generally works out for the best. The husband loves his wife so much that he would give his life for her.

When a man does not love himself due to outside circumstances, whatever they might be—stress at work, things that have followed him through his childhood, or by many other means—he does not have love inside of him that can be poured out to you. Keep this in mind as you may go through struggles in your marriage.

The Bible says that the woman is to respect her husband; it also says to submit to your own husband. This means to respect his authority. Just as love for the woman is of the utmost importance, for many men, respect is of the greatest importance. In looking at the word "respect," we can find many things. I have found six characteristics of respect that are of extreme importance: observation, esteem, courtesy, approval, honor, and attention.

NUMBER 1: OBSERVATION

You should study your husband and know every part of his body. Know every feature from his head to his toes. Does he have hair or not? How is his head shaped? How does his hair feel? What color is his hair? How does his scalp feel to your touch? Does his eye twinkle in the light of the day? What color are his eyes, and do they change color or lighten and darken with his mood?

Are there cuts or blemishes on his body? If so, how did he obtain each one? Know his neck, shoulders torso, genitals, buttocks, legs, ankles, arms—how muscular are his arms. Know his hands, his feet, and his toes. You should be able to close your eyes and see exactly what his appearance is.

Notice how he stands, how he walks, and how he talks. What are his likes and dislikes? What is his body language saying when he is happy or sad? Watch how he handles business. Look at how he relates to children and to other people.

Try looking at the world through his eyes, meaning the husband's point of view. For example, a child is riding a bike, scrapes his knee with a fall, and comes in the house crying. A female point of view may be to immediately console the child; give hugs, cleans, and kisses the scrape. The male may see a child that needs to mature and should learn to stand on his own two feet. He tells the child to go out, get back on the bike, and try it again. They handle the same situation in two completely different ways. Men and women many times see situations differently. There is no good or bad just different.

Another example is on one side, we will put the woman (wife), and over her head we will put a sign that says Love. On the other side, we will put the man (husband), and over his head, we will put a sign that says Respect.

The woman flourishes with love. For example, romance novels fly off the book shelves at book stores, and romantic movies are very popular with women. Sometimes men call them chick flicks because the movies are full of love and happy endings. This is where most women thrive. Women can give love and receive love without a second thought. Women can usually say I love you easily and frequently. That is what they need. Going back to scripture, God told the man to love. Why? Because that is what women desire—to be loved.

Men on the other side—remember the man is on the other side with a sign over his head that reads Respect. A man flourishes with respect. You can find on almost any given day a man who reads the sports page of the newspaper or who watches the football game, basketball, hockey, tennis, golf, soccer, and the many sport games available. He will hunt and fish. He watches action movies and war films. Why? Because they have to do with protecting, providing, honor, and respect. This is where he thrives. So, wives, instead of saying I love you, next time try saying I respect you. Remember, try to see things from his point of view. This is where he grows and develops. Giving him love is a good thing, but if you want to see him flourish, give him respect.

Watching your husband at work and at play can become such a pleasure. You will be surprised at the things you will learn by observing him and only him. Look for all the things you see in him to be grateful for. Is he a father that has stayed in this relationship? Is he a man that cooks dinner one or more nights a week? Does he provide shelter for his family? Does he help with cleaning the home? Does he take the children to their activities, and is he involved? Is he involved in community activities? Does he keep up and maintain the automobiles? Does he enjoy his family? Does he have quite a number of responsibilities at work? Find something in him to be grateful for. Tell him the things that you see in him that you're grateful about. Take into your thought process all the things that he does, and think with me for a moment. He does these things because he serves. He is giving, and what will he receive? It is his choice to be in the home. He stays in hopes of living life more abundantly with you.

Learn about the things that are deep within his soul. Become aware of all his ups and downs in life, the type of family life he grew up in, and how the family related to one another. Get to know all the experiences that have bought him to this place called now. Through observation, learn how to feed his soul. The soul consists of the mind, will, and emotions. To stimulate the mind would be with clever conversation. Ask him questions that are food for thought and stir up ideas. Read the paper or magazines of his favorite interest. Talk about the stories that intrigue his thought process. In feeding his will, remember the will is action. Remember when you were children? Girls had dolls and boys had action figures. Action, this means you must show him acts of respect and love. When the emotions reveal themselves, ask God for wisdom and understanding. Knowing how to nurture the many emotions that can and will arise from his soul may be challenging. Whatever they may be, let the emotions flow out and listen to him without speaking. Because once he opens up to you, how you handle this will bring you either closer and you will win his adoration, or he will shut the door on trust. Continue to feed his soul and spirit the word of God.

Number 2: Esteem

Another characteristic of respect is esteem. Through all the ups and downs in life, a wife should be knowledgeable in how to build the self-esteem of her husband. One example is to admire him. Know his attributes and tell him about them. For instance, you can tell him his muscles flex and bulge when he picks up and takes out the garbage. Touch his arms and tell him he has big strong muscles. Make sure, in admiration, that you are acknowledging his physical body. It is more effective.

One way I found to build a husband's self-esteem is to ask. I'll give you an example. I would ask my husband to go to the mall. I would say to him "Honey, may I or can I go to the mall?" For a while he just answered yes and kept doing whatever he was doing. Then one day he asked, "Why are you asking me to do these things?" I told him, "You are the head of this household, and I trust your decisions to be the correct one." He replied, "Oh, okay" with a questioning look on his face. I would ask to go to the store and if there was anything I could bring back to him. Notice I said "to him" and not "for him." The entire idea is to empower him. Some men take doing things "for him" as he is unable to do things for himself. Man thinking.

This is a wonderful way to build his self-esteem. First you ask so you are putting him in a position to make choices, in making choices, he has to make a decision. Once he can make better decisions, it builds up his confidence. As his level of confidence increases, he feels that he can do all things, which expands his mind, body and spirit.

I know right about now you are asking the question, "Why do I have to do everything? What is he going to do? Why do I have to be the one that initiates all the above?"

The Bible says that the wife is the helper to the husband. As you help him to begin to make better choices and helping him to walk into his destiny, you will find that all these things you do will generate, create, stimulate, and illuminate from within him love. You can only give what is within you. Where does a man give love? A man gives love to his wife. If you desire his love and for him to adore you, you will give, help, teach, and respect you husband.

Be considerate and play a major part in building his self-esteem. Consider things he may enjoy doing throughout the day. Is it watching a sporting event on television? Think about the things he likes that would make the experience better. Consider he has had a challenging day at work. Some men talk all day at work, so he may need a little quiet time. Before you begin to talk or the children bombard him with the day's activities, Explain to the children what quiet time is, or get a sitter for an hour, or you take the children out for a while. For some husbands, giving him some quiet time to calm down from the challenging day can bring him into the awareness of family time. This may not always be possible, but when possible, be considerate.

I will give you an example, let's call her Cheryl, Cheryl's husband is at home when she arrives. He is relaxing and listening to music. The music is softly playing; he is nice and relaxed, enjoying being who he is. Cheryl walks in the door in a rush, turns on the television, and turns off the music. She had a television show she wanted to watch. Let's look at this another way. Cheryl enters the house and hears the music playing. She sees that his is relaxing or maybe even almost asleep. She greets him, considering what mood he is in, but she really wants to watch the television show. Cheryl can tape it to see it later, or ask him if it's all right to watch her favorite show. Cheryl, saying, "Sweetheart, if it's okay with you, I would like to turn the music off so I can hear better." Also remember to say *thank you*.

Another way you can build his self-esteem is to pay tribute to him. Recognize him as the head of the household, the husband and/or father. Giving you an example, Dana chose one day of the month to be Ron's, her husband, day. Whatever her husband wanted to do, that became the events of the day. They would attend sports games or watch them on TV together. No matter what it was, she would sit and watch it with him. Go out to breakfast, brunch, or dinner.

All things in the day surround him. For instance, if Dana's friend would call, instead of talking, Dana would tell her friend, "This is Ron's day, so I will call you tomorrow," *Click.*

The best way to describe a tribute to him would be praise manifested by any act—a poem, a letter, a song, gifts, a party or celebration with just the two of you or many friends and family. Be creative as so many wives are. We multitask every day, and if you feel that you cannot find a creative bone in your being, ask for help. Have you ever heard the saying that when a student is ready to learn, the teacher will show up? Believe.

Paying tribute to him lets him know how special he is in your life. He feels important and respected. You can help him come into a place of a higher awareness. This can stimulate love within him.

NUMBER 3: COURTESY

Wives, in our day-to-day to-do list, which can include our "honey-do" list, we get concerned with trying to accomplish all the items on our list and can seldom remember to be polite and gracious.

It is easy to forget to say, "Thank you," "Excuse me, is there anything I can get you?" "Do you have anything that you desire?" And a simple "How I can help you?"

Think about a high-end retail store. When you enter, the atmosphere there is an air of graciousness. Everyone is polite and friendly. It takes only moments before someone will ask how they may serve you. Whether you make a purchase or not, you will receive a thank you. It is a place of service with a smile. You leave with a feeling of well-being.

Let me give you an example. Friends of mine took a vacation to the Hawaiian Islands. They stayed in one of the best hotels on the island. When they drove up to the hotel, the valet service took their keys and gave them the keys to their room. They did not go to a desk to check in, and everyone in the hotel called them by name. All the services were top-of-the-line, and the facilities were a place to enjoy and relax. As they entered the lobby, there was a huge room that invited them to sit and enjoy the beauty of life. In their room, they could push a button, and the Do Not Disturb sign would appear on their door and in the bathroom, there was a full window for a view of the island. In there, not only could they take a bath with a view, but at a touch of a button, the glass would frost so they could not see out, and no one could see into the bathroom. This is the best in customer service. Courtesy can go hand in hand with great service.

Can you as a wife find times throughout your day that you show a spirit of service toward your husband?

I was shopping, and the customer in front of me in the check-out line became loud and irate and downright disrespectful. The customer called for a manager, and when the manager arrived, the manager listened to the problem, and even though the customer was wrong, the manager was very tactful and gave the reason on how the company solved problems. Using tact with the customer calmed the customer down and resolved the problem.

I remember once, I was hanging clothes in our closet and became frustrated. The closet was packed with clothing and I had to hang and straighten each item of clothing. When my husband would hang clothes he would hang each item and not straighten each item so the clothing would be extremely wrinkled. I asked my husband, "Do you know how to hang up clothes?" This wife was not using tact. Like many commercials say, "Do not try this at home." This was not the best way to handle this situation, but frustration caused me to act without thinking. Another way of handling this would have been to say, "Honey, how do you hang up clothes in the closet? I would like to learn how you hang them so we will know how to bring our two different styles together." When you ask the first way he may hear, "She thinks I do not know what I am doing, I am inadequate I am not living up to her standards, she does not trust me, I am not good enough." Understand not all men will think this way, but remember to think about different ways to say things to him that build him up and leave him feeling like a man.

Sometimes things do not go quite as planned, or husbands and wives disagree. When this occurs, stop and think first, you must be calm because at times like this you may need to use tact instead of striking out, man bashing, and using loud and foul language.

Being a wife does require knowing how to be tactful. For some wives, this can be as natural as breathing, and for some of us, it can take the experience of time and hard knocks to learn and acquire this skill. Tact is having the skill to deal with your husband in a difficult situation, in such a delicate way that you can avoid being offensive.

Grace is a virtue, one that can be acquired. Study and dig for answers needed that will help you become the wife that he deserves.

NUMBER 4: APPROVAL

Men enjoy compliments from their wives. A complement is like a stamp of approval. It lets him know he is the best of men. A wife knows her husband better than and deeper than anyone else. He exudes love to her. Her approval means more to him then anything that anyone else could say.

For example, a man goes to the gym daily. He takes great care of his body, watches his weight, and is concerned about his health. Everyone in the gym can tell him he has built a great body. Coworkers can tell him and notice that he works out, but when he comes home to his *queen*, his wife, and she says, "Oooh, you have big muscles, what a great body you have, my love." Everything in him lights up. He may blush and smile all day. He thinks, "Yeah, she noticed all this work I do for her, to keep that twinkle in her eye." He does this to be happy and healthy, to be here with you and/or with the children for a long time.

Because men are driven to be providers, they will work long grueling hours. He takes the pressure of a demanding boss and coworkers that can sap all the energy out of him. Sometimes commuting long distances through hours of traffic and the road rage of other drivers. The husband does this on almost a daily basis to fulfill the need to be the provider of his family. He is doing the man thing.

If you would like to know what a day is like in his world, ask if you can accompany him one day to see what his work is all about, how he spends the day to provide for his family. Doing this can give you an idea of what your husband goes through daily. If you cannot be with him in a day at work, ask lots of questions about what his day was like; listen and check every day for a week.

Once you get a glance of what he goes through every day, learn how to cheer him on. In most workplaces and daily routines, it is rare to get a pat on the back or "You did an excellent job," or "I appreciate you." When he comes home to a place of refuge, cheer him on. You heard on the news that there was an accident on the freeway this evening, and it took him an extra hour and a half to get home. There are things you can say like "Honey, you are such a strong man, you sat on the freeway for hours in traffic, your patience is unbreakable. If you can do that, I believe you can do anything." A few simple words can bring new life into a tired soul.

Applaud his successes when he receives the position he desired and worked so hard to get. He made it to the gym every day before or after work. Each time he came to the children's activities or when he goes that extra mile, applaud him; tell him how proud you are of him. Tell him you are so happy and/or excited for him. Do something special purchase a gift, give him and encouragement card. Call him in the middle of the day with encouraging words from the deepest depths of your heart. Let the fruit of your lips bless him.

Husbands can come up with numerous ideas. When he does, let him know you are with him. Remember the wife is the helper. You can stand with him or you can stand for him. If you have the desire to see him do wondrous things, stand up and give your approval.

Show him you are going to be there, sink or swim. The Bible says when you have done all you can do, stand. Let him in his mind and imagination see you standing with him. Let him see you standing through his challenging times. Let him see you standing for him saying, "Honey, you can do all things through Christ, I believe in you, you are more than a conqueror, I am here with you all the way. Keep going, keep moving forward."

Give your prayers and your blessing. Bless him coming and bless his going out. Ask him if there is anything he wants you to pray for him today. Be a blessing. Be a wife.

NUMBER 5: HONOR

Give him credit where credit is due. In giving honor to him, make sure you always speak highly of your husband in private and in public. One woman in front of her children told her husband, "Thank you for always giving me the best car to drive. You take good care of us, and thank you so much, it means so much to me. You are a wonderful husband and father."

Can you imagine the impact on the entire family? The husband feels extremely honored and beams with joy. The wife receives more love, the children learn how to respect there father and adore their mother. It is a win-win situation. When you can tell someone else, with your husband present, "I love my husband, he is a wonderful man." He hears you esteem him to others. To him this is an honorable gesture. Think about war movies. When they show honor, they award a medal, all the other soldiers are present when the commander presents the Medal of Honor. Honor is not something done in the closet it is done out in front, in the open, for all to see.

Think of ways to honor him more than just for Father's Day or birthdays because anyone anywhere can celebrate on these days. The difference of honoring him on different days is then he knows this is all just for him. It can warm is heart in knowing he is doing well for his wife and family. Theses are new pictures to play over and over in his mind, encouraging him through the day and night. Knowing that you honor his presence is one of the greatest gifts you can ever give to your husband.

Honor you husband because you care about him because you love him, just because he is a wonderful loving father, because he stands as the head of the home, and because of your love for God.

NUMBER 6: ATTENTION

Attention is having consciousness, care, and curiosity of your husband. Be conscious of what may be on his mind. Maybe it is a project at work. Men can be very analytical, and he may be thinking about all the resources available to complete a project. He can become distant or stressed. Anxiety is at its highest peak. Recognize what his needs are.

Ask if there is any way you can help him.

You can see him grind his teeth, or the tension in his jaw and his shoulder muscles are tight. Now is a good time for a refreshing drink and a hot bath with relaxing lavender or lavender mix aromatherapy. Put a dimmer switch in the bathroom to dim the lights or use candles to put him into the relaxed mode. You can join him in the bath and talk about happy and joyous times or not talk at all.

Purchase a towel warmer, or put the towels into the dryer until it is time to exit the bath. The towels will be warm and relaxing, helping to soothe the mind and body.

Give him a massage. An upper-body or a full-body massage can bring total bliss at the end of a hectic day.

Having thoughts of consciousness about what he is thinking, what is on his mind at the time of whatever situation may arise, what can you do that can help you better care for him and/or his body?

What does his body desire at this time? Is it food, drink, to become relaxed? Is it sleep or sex? Curiosity is finding out what is going to feed his spirit. Understand what kind words can do. Play uplifting music, and the two of you dance around the room or give him huge heartfelt hug. Let him know what it is like to lie in your arms on your breast for comfort. Pay conscious attention to his mind, body, and spirit.

All of these six characteristics are joined together to create the magnificent word— respect. Remember observation, esteem, courtesy, approval, honor, and attention. A woman's strength is being willing and capable of giving her husband what he desires, and one of his greatest desires is to be respected. You can find respect without love, but with true love, you will find respect.

Women of today are very independent. We have careers; we can take care of children and all the activities that can come along with the responsibility of being a mom—football-team mom, soccer mom, dance classes, cheer practice, etc. Women care for their homes and entertain family and friends. We solve problems and put out fires that pop up everywhere each day. With schedules like this, it is difficult to think of what love really means.

Throughout our lives, we have heard God is love.

In 1 Corinthians 13:1-8 reads, "Though I speak with the tongues of men and of angels, but have not love, I have become sounding brass or a clanging cymbal. And though I have the *gift of prophecy*, and understand all mysteries and all knowledge, and though I have all faith, so that I could remove mountains, but have not love, I am nothing. And through I bestow all my goods to feed *the poor*, and though I give my body to be burned, but have not love, it profits me nothing. Love suffers long *and* is kind; love does not envy; love does not parade itself, is not puffed up; does not behave rudely, does not seek its own, is not provoked, thinks no evil; does not rejoice in iniquity, but rejoices in the truth; bears all things, believes all things, hopes all things, endures all things. Love never fails.

Looking at this, there is no question why so many people desire love. Over time, we must learn how to give and most importantly to receive love. When there is love inside your heart, it is easy to give away. But first you must acquire love for yourself. Learn how to love yourself and be true to yourself. Know what love has got to do with it for you.

Once you come into the wisdom, knowledge, and understanding of love and can operate in giving love and receiving love—especially receiving love—you have now chosen to surrender to love.

Part 2

ONE FLESH

The Bible says in Genesis 2:21-24

And the Lord God caused a deep sleep to fall on Adam, and he slept; and He took one of his ribs, and closed up the flesh in its place. Then the rib which the Lord God had taken from man He made into a woman, and He brought her to the man. And Adam said: "This is now bone of my bones and flesh of my flesh; She shall be called Woman, because she was taken out of Man." Therefore a man shall leave his father and mother and be joined to his wife, and they shall become one flesh. (NKJV)

The Bible says shall become one flesh. At the time you marry, you begin the journey of becoming one flesh. Becoming one flesh is work.

When you think of two becoming one, you think about two separate people, to combine their lives together to become one. Their lives are mixed together in a relationship that is so strong, nothing can come between them. Nothing can pull them apart. Remember your vows (let no man separate). If you were to mix two things together, you will no longer be able to see the beginning of one or the end of the other. This brings to mind the ring you wear on your finger. It is an infinite circle; you cannot find the beginning or find the end, it is a continuous circle. There is no greater symbol for marriage than the ring.

It is like baking a cake. When you bake a cake, you gather all the ingredients together—eggs milk, butter, sugar (this is not a box cake), flour, your flavoring, etc. You put them in a mixing bowl to mix your ingredients together. Now when you mix it together, you agitate the mixture to get it all to combine. If you look at the recipe, it would say beat mixture until well blended. There are things that can enter into your relationship that will agitate you both. Your greatest agitation will come from family and friends. For instance, his parents may want you to be with them for the holidays, and your parents want you to be with them. Family can pull and tug at the marriage. Especially when they say, "You want to be with them more than with us." If you let it, this can become a huge quarrel between the two of you and or between the families. Friends may say now that you are married, and you do not have freedom. Or they may say now you have a ball and chain. Believe me; these friends do not know what the marriage that was designed by God is really like. Bending two lives together is a process. It is process that last a lifetime. Remember your vows (until death do us part). So agitation can bring you closer together. Then you put it—the cake—in the oven under some heat, and the heat causes the cake mixture to change form. The *mixture* rises, swells, and gets larger and fluffier. When the cake comes out of the oven, it is a new thing. It becomes a good thing. A cake that is sweet and inviting. Once it has cooled, you put the icing on the cake and enjoy. You cannot pull out the eggs once it has been mixed or baked. You cannot separate the ingredients now. Over time and through changing conditions, it has transformed.

Let me give you an example from my life. When my husband and I got married, it was like when worlds collide. His family did things a certain way and my family did things a certain way. For instance, he liked the toilet paper to come from under the roll, and I liked the toilet paper to come from on top of the roll. He came out of the bathroom one day and said to me, "Don't you know how to put the toilet paper on the spindle? It comes from the bottom of the roll." I said, "I like the toilet paper to come from the top of the roll." He said, "My mother taught us the right way, and the paper is supposed to come from the bottom." Right about now, if we were on TV, there would be a message that scrolls across the bottom of the screen that would read Do Not Try This at Home. I know you can imagine what my reaction was. He played the "mother card". So we argued about toilet paper, and when all was said and done, we decided that the person who puts the new roll on can put it on the way that's preferred. We sometimes went back-and-forth where we would change the roll anyway we liked it. Then the children came along, and after a while, it was no longer an issue because all we wanted to know is do we have toilet paper. Our thoughts joined and became one. Thoughts are blended together, creating the standards that we live by.

Keep in mind that when your husband talks about his mother constantly and brings up all the things that she does, he loves his mother. It is wonderful that he loves her so because the same way he talks about her to you will be the same way he would talk about you to others. If your husband only had a mother in the home, that is all he knows, and he may not get the full understanding of how a household is ran when there is a husband and wife present. Know that he is trying to help you in the only way he knows how. He is trying to help you solve a problem. This is a man's analytical thinking way of solving an issue he sees that you are trying to solve. You must guide him into a better way of saying and doing things for you, and believe me, he probably does not have a clue.

When you leave your father and mother's house, you create a new house. It takes time and patience. Take the best of both worlds; mix them together to create what is best for both of you. Have you ever met a couple that say the same thing the same way, or he will start a sentence and she will end the sentence, or overtime the couple begins to look alike? Well you are looking at a couple that is in the process of creating one flesh. It does not matter if the teamwork started years ago or starts today, it is a lifetime commitment. The Bible also says that this is a great mystery. So becoming one flesh is a puzzle that both of you will solve together.

There was this story I heard when I was a little girl about a king, and when he married, he found that his wife was unfaithful, so he killed her, and he decided that that would never happen to him again. So he would marry and have a wedding night and at the rising of the sun, the wife had to give up her life. This went on for some time, and he desired this one woman named Scheherazade for his wife. On the wedding night, she told him a story that intrigued him, and at the rising of the sun, she was at the best part of the story, so he let her live another day to continue the story she told so well. She went on night after night. The story goes on to say that she lived for many years and eventually had children with him. Overtime he began to love her. He adored her, and his feelings of love were so strong for her that she escaped the law of death that he had put into place. Why was she so different from all the other women before her? She did not survive because of her beauty. I am sure all of his wives were beautiful. It was not because of the sex. He had sex with all the wives. This woman knew something powerful. Scheherazade was able to feed her husbands soul. She was a very wise and skillful in being a wife. She had the ability to calm him down. A soothing of his soul to the point, where he becomes open. She won his trust. Now is the time to talk to him about life, love, etc. You can help him come into a place of a higher awareness. This intimacy stimulates love within your husband.

In the skill of feeding your husband's soul, we know that the soul contains the mind, the will, and the emotions. In his mind, she was able to cause him to think; once he started thinking and analyzing, he began to create. He was in a creative process and became challenged. He would now, in his mind, reason, believe, reflect, and live with expectancy.

To give you an example, remember when you were a child and you learned the alphabet song.

ABCDEFG,
HIJKLMNOP,
QRS,
TUV,
WXY and Z
Now I know my ABC's
Next time won't you sing with me?

This was a song you sang all day. It was fun and gave you a feeling of joy and happiness. You would dance or sway a little when you sang and encouraged others to join you in the next choirs of the song. At the time, you did not know that you were learning your alphabet, something that you would use every day of your life. When you were putting something in alphabetical order, you would go back to that song. You learned something that would be your greatest ways of communication. This was something that had endless possibilities.

You can also look at the Bible. There are many stories that teach, instruct, and cause us to think. The stories help us to understand life and to meditate to seek direction and a deeper understanding of who we are.

In the part of him that is his will, it will give him a strong and fixed purpose. He will begin to have the power to make a choice or a decision and control his own actions. The will is more of an action. Like the "I do" in your wedding vows. As in Philippians 2:13 (for it is God who works in you both to will and to do for *His* good pleasure), God works in the will and to do—again, will and do are words of action. What actions will you take with what you now know? What will you do with the information? How can this bring about change? In the story, the king took action and started to love and trust again. The change was she has now created the ability to save her life. The king was able to do the right thing in the correct way, to love his family.

In the part of the emotions, she could raise strong feelings. Now feelings have a flip side; you can touch the bad feelings—such as, guilt, shame, anger, unworthiness—or you can touch the good feelings—happiness, joy, love, laughter, and so on. When your husband begins to think and his will is to do something and the emotions behind the action are on the surface regardless of what they are, be thoughtful. Life and death is in the power of the tongue. It is up to you to choose life. Speak only positive things to him, about him, and with him. Wives, you can acquire the skill of feeding his soul. It will take thought and patience.

I would like to give to you some interesting techniques to apply to your life as a wife. My bishop would say sometimes;" some of you women need to learn how to talk to a man. I would scratch my head and turn it to the side in thought. What does this mean? Here is what I found. First you must develop a softer voice. You can develop a voice that caresses his ears as well as his soul. Remove the harsh tones that have been created by your experiences in the world. This is an acquired skill of a wife. It will take time and lots of practice. Say your husband name over and over; notice how it sounds to your ears, repeat it over and over until you hear a softer sound in the tone of your voice. Something that sounds peaceful, and inviting. This is not a seductive voice; you will use this voice every day. It becomes part of you just as living the life of a wife.

The smile on your face should be seen in your eyes. When he walks into a room, does he see the light in your eyes as you welcome him into your space? Have happy eyes.

Also I have talked with quite a few women, and their husbands would say to them, "It's all about you. You don't care about anyone but yourself." I knew these women, and they were completely in love with their husbands and wanted their marriages to grow.

I asked them to write a love letter to their husbands, and I'd like to see it before they give it to them. I would like to invite you to write a love letter to your husband now. Stop reading and begin to write your letter of love to him. After you have written the letter, come back and start your reading again. Stop and write. It was very common for the wife to say, "I love you. I know that you are the only one for me," or "I think about you all the time." Or "I remember when . . ."

From a man's eyes and ears, he hears "I," meaning "you." So every time you said "I," he sees and hears it as you are talking about yourself. Now let's do this another way. Instead of I love you, a different way would be to say, "Honey, you are so loved." When he hears this, you are putting him first, and you are talking about him not yourself. When you say, "I think you are the only one for me." Another way to say it would be to say;" you are the only one for me." I think about you all the time and another way to say that would be to say" You are the thought of the day you big hunk of man." I remember when can be changed to "remember when. Change as many I's into you or eliminate the I's all together. Think about how things look from his point of view. Put yourself in his shoes and become aware of how your husband thinks. How does your letter look? Can you word a few things differently? Now rewrite the letter and include a few rose petals or sprinkle confetti. Spray on your favorite fragrance or add stickers to your heart felt words of love.

I would like to bring to your attention one concept. The Bible tells us to love God and to love our neighbors as you love yourself. You create a healthy and/or Godly love for yourself. Remember the law of first within then without. Work on your inside with things like reading the word of God and inspirational books. Give your time to things that will encourage and build your spirit. Attend workshops for women or conferences that can inspire you.

Enjoy time set aside for yourself. Women are usually so giving that they give time to everyone else and then do not have enough time to give to themselves. On the outside, have a Queen Esther moment. Enjoy taking a bath with oils and rose petals, candles, and/or soothing music. Take time out to rub fragrant oils and lotions into your skin to stay soft and smooth. Get as much rest as your schedule will allow. Because with sleep, your body replenishes and heals itself; you will feel better with plenty of rest. Take care of your skin, hair, and nails. Brush your hair or let him have the pleasure of brushing your hair for you.

You can care for your nails either professionally or yourself. There are many professionals our there that will teach you how to take care of your hair and nails on your own. Get help in areas where you feel you don't have a clue. If it's clothing style, health care, everyday etiquette, shopping of any kind, skin care, voice lessons, hair removal, dental care or teeth whitening, eye care glasses versus contacts; try eyelashes, exercise to sculpt your body. Encourage and give to yourself first so you will have enough in you to give to others.

Celebrate being feminine. Men enjoy seeing a woman that carries herself as a feminine female, a woman. That's one of the things that men take pleasure in—the difference between men and women. When your husband looks deep into your beautiful eyes, he sees a reflection of himself. You are a reflection of your husband. Men will also see you as feminine when you wear flowers or girly prints. Many women have experienced this along with me. There are lots of women today that are businesswomen and have a professional lifestyle and they dress accordingly. Many women in business wear business suits every day—at work, business suit; at church, a business suit. To a party or out to dinner with their husbands, need I say a business suit or a professional look? Try wearing a feminine dress and (maybe with flowers) and see his reaction. If he enjoys the flowers, you may want to include a few new items in your wardrobe to give his eyes something to enjoy.

Some women choose to make themselves accustomed to wearing pants all the time. Become more feminine by trying to dress in dresses or skirts, something that is made especially for your more girly side. Purchase accessories like earrings, bracelets, rings and belts and pins to accessorize your outfits. Have an adventure day to discover what perfume or fragrance delights you senses. I understand and can relate. I myself do not like flowers or anything with a girly print. When I forced myself to purchase a summer dress with flowers, I would get embarrassed at the thought. The dress stayed in the closet for weeks, then I gathered my courage and wore the dress. My husband saw the dress and said, "You look so beautiful. I like that dress." And I felt so silly in this flowered dress. I asked myself, "How can he like this dress?" But the dress was what I call a girly dress, and he loved it. Some men like their wives to look like innocent little girls. Someone they can protect and care for.

When you look like a businesswoman and have that professional appearance, to a man, you look like you can take care of yourself. If you can take care of yourself, you have just put him out of a job. Remember, he is a provider and protector by design. He wants to take care of you. In his heart, he wants to provide for you, so you must learn to let a man be a man. Give him opportunity to do what he has been created to do.

Be careful of becoming a manipulator. There is a fine line between helping and controlling. It can be easy for you to take control of any situation or want him to do things your way or no way at all. Using these techniques to control him into doing what you want is not appropriate.

When issues arise, and they will, lay all the things you believe out on the table with an explanation. Let him make the final decision even though you may think another way is better. He may need to make mistakes to learn how to trust your decisions and/or opinions. When he makes a mistake, be a gracious wife. Talk to him in private about his decision and what you both can do now to correct or chalk it up to experience and move on. Challenging his decisions in front of the children or in front of other friends or family and even other people can crush and dissolve his leadership.

My life experience with this issue was this. One day at one of my son's football games, I stood up and told everybody who would listen that I wore the pants in our family, and that I was the boss. Everyone laughed and joked about it. It was all in fun. Little did I know that I had just humiliated my husband. I belittled him and snatched the king off his throne. I told everyone that he was not a good provider; he could not protect or lead his family. Well, I really stepped in the you-know-what on that one. I did go back to make things right. Not right away because for a while I did not know what to do. Understanding what I had done all these years eventually came crashing down on me, and I decided to do things through God's way. It was difficult because it was so different from what I was accustomed to. It was a daily challenge. Many days I tried to apologize with no action. The words would not come out of my mouth. I was stuck. I had become stuck in pride. I did not want to be the peacemaker or the one to start this new way of life. Days turned into weeks, and weeks turned into months, and I finally—through practice, I might add—was able to put everything into words. I said, "Honey, I am sorry for embarrassing you and not respecting your authority as the man of this house. You have put up with my bad behavior for such a long time, and I am truly sorry. Please forgive me. Because of what is in our past, I know that you are a strong and faithful husband, and from now on,

I will be the wife that someone like you deserves." This time the words finally came out. We were then able to go on and start anew. We became much closer and continued our journey in becoming one flesh.

As much as you work on the outside, work on the inside more. Let your outward appearance reflect what is on the inside of you. Be a loving peacemaker and refuse to play games. Do not let anything tear you apart, not even pride. Let the fruit of your lips bless your husband. One last word, smile.

Part 3

THE BATTLES WE FIGHT

The battles we fight in fighting for our marriages are not always with your husband. Many of the battles are with you, the battles you fight and struggle with every day of your life. These are battles that are fought within you. No one can see the hurt and pain or the trauma you've had to face. Other people cannot see the wounds created by each and every act against you. They cannot see the cuts or bleeding of your heart. These are your secrets, buried in a hole that you have been trying to dig your way out of for quite some time, only to find yourself looking up and recognizing you are even deeper in the hole than before. You try to climb out of that dark hole, feeling the earth crumble as you grasp it in your hands. Through the tears and cries for help, you can become extremely exhausted. Now there is a decision to make: Will you continue to have hope and keep climbing, or will you lie back and wait for them to cover you up in your grave. A grave that has been dug by your past, and whether you realize it or not, your secrets affect your future.

There are millions of women that have felt and are still fighting the battle of physical abuse, mental abuse, sexual abuse, and infidelity.

Sexual abuse is when a child or a person is exploited by another person or, in the case of a child, an older person for the satisfaction of the abuser's needs.

Being sexually abused as a child is one of the most devastating things that can happen in your life. This can affect the relationship you have with your husband in ways we will discuss later.

Many times the abuser is someone close to you that you, as a child, love and trust. Someone you believe will protect you at all cost and would give their life for you. Family members—a father, a brother, an uncle, a grandfather or stepfather or stepgrandfather, it could be a cousin or a close friend of the family. Sometimes it's the people that have easy access to or have private time with a child, like a teacher, a coach, or a counselor.

Every person's experience is unique. Not all survivors suffer the same way. The abuse can come in different ways. Verbal abuse is when someone makes lewd remarks or talks sexually about your body. When you begin to develop, and the hormones are running wild any way, this can be a detrimental to a child's development. The decisions they make that can lead them either to success or into destructive behavior.

Visual abuse is when someone exposes you, as a child, to pornography or acts of exhibitionism. Acts that people feel are totally innocent, like taking a bath with your child of the opposite sex well into their years of elementary school, can and will have its effects. Whether it is live and in living color or it is on the screen, it will play in your mind like a movie over and over. In your sleep the movie will play; while you are at school the movie will play; in all the things you experience, you will still see the pictures. The way you visualize life has now been altered. You may become an actor in the movie, or you might choose to run as far away as you can, choosing not to live your life and the reality it causes that will affect you.

Physical abuse is when someone fondles private parts of the child's body or has oral sex with the child or intercourse and penetration of any kind. By far this is the most damaging, and recovery can take as long as a lifetime. Usually in physical abuse, the abuses are all rolled into one, magnifying your experience.

The effects of the abuse can cause more damage if it occurs frequently or over a long time. The closer the abuser is to you, the greater the damage. The wider the age difference or abuse involving penetration of any kind is more harmful. If you were, as a child, subject to sadistic or violent abuse, or if you told someone and there was no response and you did not get the help you so desperately cried out for, the greater the damage.

These things can affect you before and after your marriage in one way or another. One way is that in your mind, things have been distorted. You can believe that relationships are not safe; therefore, you run from or cannot commit to men. All the men you choose to spend time with are either going through a divorce and still have a constant relationship with their wives, or someone that cannot commit to you as you desire. An example of a man that is distant is a workaholic husband. He is so busy with everything else in his life that he never has time for you. You may be confused trying to figure out if relationships with others are good or bad. You build walls and defense mechanisms because you have got to be always strong and protect yourself. Because if you become vulnerable, you are setting yourself up for even more hurt and pain. You pretend that everything is okay, and life is perfect, but inside you feel that you are not worthy of any good thing.

This is a battle of unworthiness and/or not being good enough. In this place is where you can find women that are overachievers. These women will climb the ladder of success quickly. Instead of one business, she will have two or three. Multitasking is taken to the next level and into hyperdrive. She can work well into the night and rise early the next day to begin the cycle all over again. She looks for perfection in all that she sees. Everything can be done better. She will strive to be the best, not understanding where the drive of perfection comes from. It can be a cry for approval, or for the love she desired, but never felt worthy enough to receive. She continually and desperately seek to find that one think that says, "You are okay." Everybody knows that if you are perfect and you please everyone, they will love you. You feel that you will be loved and valued more than anyone else. What you need is a mirror that does not show the distortions like the one at the amusement parks. You need a mirror that is crystal clear, one that allows you freedom from what has been created in your past. The vision of seeing yourself looking toward a brighter future you will find out later is yours for the asking.

Once you grow into adulthood, there can be after effects. You will hate your body. Your destructive behavior emerges, like not caring about what you eat. You may not eat at all (anorexia), or you may eat and throw up (bulimia). You hate the way you look. So you will never have mirrors around, or you will not see yourself as you look in it. Some women will not be able to look at her reflection in the mirror. If you were to ask her what she sees in the mirror, she might reply nothing. Building self-esteem is almost impossible. Many women choose to gain enormous amounts of weight, thinking that men will never bother them again and they can live in peace. Fat becomes your protection. It is the wall you have secretly chosen for comfort.

You can attach yourself to addictions very easily. Food will be your best friend, and you will eat to soothe your soul. If the food does not taste good, you will find other ingredients to make it taste the way you want it. More butter, more sugar, and more gravy. Every time that movie plays in your head, just like at the movie theater, you have got to have something to eat. The food intoxicates you, and sometimes you have got to have a full stomach to go to sleep. In your mind, food is love. You live to eat instead of eating to live.

Drugs can become a big part of your life. Not just illegal drugs, but you may begin to take too many sleeping pills because you cannot sleep. This might be because your abuser came to you in the night in the past. Your mind still reacts to the event thus causing you to be restless and not getting a sound nights sleep.

Sexual addiction—you have and desire sex when you just want to feel loved. You want to feel good over and over; it is not about the sex, it is about how it makes you feel. Sometimes it can be to have what you want and to control the sexual situation, it makes you feel better. Sexual situations can go to extremes, from sexual addition to never having a desire to engage in any sexual act. This can go from prostitution to being an old maid. Understand how one incident can affect your life forever.

You may have suicidal tendencies of just wanting to end it all, and in your mind, dying becomes better than living. You just want the pain inside to end or for your mind to finally rest. This can occur over and over at different times in your life and can be bought on by stress or times of high anxiety. You can have self-mutilation tendencies that can include cutting one's self. This can occur on any part of the body, including the genital area. The pain of the cuts help to take away or distract your mind from the pain your soul feels. The hurt of the shame is so strong that you may feel it is the only way out. Just maybe one day you will pass out and never wake up because you know that there has got to be a better way to live than this.

You can experience sleeping disorders. I can tell you how this affected my sleeping habits. When I got married, it was very difficult to sleep with my husband. I was very restless and would sleep only for a short time. When he went off to work, I would crash and sleep like a baby. As years went by, I recognized what was happening and went for counseling. It helped somewhat, but I still would not sleep until the rising of the sun. I would always take long naps in the daytime because I would not and could not sleep through the night. There were times I used bottles and bottles of sleeping pills to make me sleep through the night; sometimes it worked and sometimes it did not. I began taking three pills then four and decided this was not working for me. When I was asleep, and my husband would touch me, I would pull away and sometimes sit straight up in the bed and scream. My body automatically reacted to what had happened to me in the past. When stress and anxiety were at their highest, the symptoms would intensify. With no rest, your body will begin to break down, your immune system will be compromised, and you will get ill.

In the emotional department, you can suffer from anger. The slightest thing can set you off, or you may not be able to let go of the anger in a situation because a person made you angry. Fear can raise its ugly head, causing you to not want to go out at night or be alone or to be around a crowd of people. Depression can cause appetite changes, causing weight loss or gain. It can also cause drastic mood swings. Your husband will not know who are. He may ask, "Are you my wife today, or are you the crazy wife?" Depression can cause great sadness or hopelessness at times. You cannot concentrate and will have little or no energy. You can experience overwhelming guilt. An example could be is that you may have person that bumps into you; they say I'm sorry instead of excuse me, but they find themselves saying I'm sorry all day. Numbness can come over you, and you will turn off your emotions. You walk around like a zombie; you tell yourself that you are not going to feel anything. "No matter what it is, I will not feel it." Because as a child, when you asked for help and do not receive it or nobody comes to your rescue, you must learn how to protect yourself. When the abuser comes to get you, you have got to protect yourself, and the only way a child can do this is to shut down. That is why you can only remember the color of the bed or sofa or only remember the surroundings and not the act itself.

Your thinking changes, and feelings of unworthiness can consume you. You wonder if there is really a God and why did he not help you. You can believe that God is not real and he surely cannot protect you. Then you spend your life trying to do everything yourself—protecting yourself, caring for yourself with words like "Nobody helped me, why should I help someone else." You believe that there is nothing called love. Love does not exist. You don't know what it is, but you will find yourself looking for it, and you do not know or understand that you are looking for when all the time you are looking for love.

You have been taught about betrayal been rejected, humiliated and abandoned. Lies and deceit are what you are familiar with, and they become your closest friends. It will become impossible for you to trust. You will not trust a man or a woman, your

This is my outline on a book called Being A Wife. Living the life of a wife. It's for adults who are married or wish to become one day.

Audience: is for adults who have been married a long time or wish to have a long successful marriage.

Writing the author uses awesome vocabulary. this is a book that everyone could relate too. whether your married or not.

publication Xlibris corporation, the author

September 30, 2009

Wednesday

7 am	
8 00	
9 00	
10 00	
11 00	
12 pm	

pastor, or your boss, and the greatest ones are that you will not trust is your husband and God.

The effects of abuse can go on for years. If you recognize some of the things you do, or if you cannot see them and others can, now is the time to come closer to God. Continue to *pray* and follow the direction of getting help. Abuse is something you cannot overcome by yourself because if you could, you would have done it by now.

Physical abuse, where you were continually beaten as a child or if you have experienced it as an adult, will have the same effects as sexual abuse. We can make excuses and hide the scars. You stay locked in the house until all the bruises heal. You can cover some up with cosmetics, but sometimes, healing of the mind can take longer. When you can feel the pain inside, and it hurts so badly, eventually you become numb to the pain and all emotions. It is like a burn; when it is so deep, for a moment you cannot feel the pain. Then it begins to heal, and the pain changes into the torture of your emotions. You may be experiencing it now in the relationship with you husband. Get help! Keep reaching out until you find an answer. Pray and let God direct you and bring you into a better life with him. Please get help. Not only does your soul cry out, but your body lives with constant fear and pain. Make a plan today. The number for the national domestic violence hotline is 1-800-799-7233.

Mental abuse, a constant beating you get with words. Mind games of the worst kind. This acts the same as sexual abuse. The effects on your life are very similar and sometimes more intense, depending on the depth of the abuse and when it began. You are attacked in your mind. For some of us, it is daily and for others not as often, but enough to damage your way of thinking. Mental abuse causes great confusion. You will look at your life through prison bars. Bars that even if they were removed, you will have a difficult time walking out of the cell, because you feel that you can never be free, it is impossible to enjoy freedom. Life is distorted and can be very challenging to overcome.

If you have experienced all of the above, know that your damage is greater than most. Sometimes the three go hand in hand. All abuse can leave the same residue. It will take more time and patience to overcome. The good news is that you can overcome any situation. It's like peeling an onion. The outer layer is hard and brittle, but as you continue to peel the onion, the fragrance begins to rise. Your eyes will start to burn, and tears will emerge. You won't be able to control the tears, and your body is naturally reacting to the fragrance. You begin to peel off hate, anger, resentment, along with shame, humiliation and the feelings of unworthiness. As you peel the onion, the skin gets softer. The center of the onion is the part of the onion that regenerates and recreates. If you let an onion sit for a while, you will see a sprout come up through the center. The onion will recreate itself and has the potential of creating many others like itself. The possibilities are endless. Through the process of peeling off the layers you will find peace that you did not know existed. From peace, joy will emerge; your self control may become stronger. Things you could not do before are easier to accomplish. The new work-out program and weight loss you have been imagining becomes an accomplishment. You can move from eye glasses to contacts. You stop eating so much; you drink in moderation as depression falls away into your past. Your personality may become softer and gentleness can be seen as part of your attributes. You find time for yourself as you begin to discover who you are. Rest becomes a welcoming friend. In this place you are renewing your mind and have a new way of thinking. You can recreate yourself. Creating a unique person that is opening up for an exciting life. You finally get to the part of you what is fully open. Welcoming love into your life and after a while being able to give love. When you find love, you will know that your search has ended. You will know that you have found what you have been looking for all your life—true love.

INFIDELITY: A BATTLE THAT A MARRIAGE CAN SURVIVE

Infidelity can begin in number of ways, but the usual or most common are feelings of loneliness. Loneliness can be caused by many of the abuse issues discussed earlier. The mind has a distorted view of life, and the no-one-really-cares-about-me attitude. This could be true because if he married a woman that has shut down her feelings, he may be correct in the way he is feeling. Your husband can also need an ego boost. This is one reason you want to try feeding his soul. Then again, some men truly love their wives but continue to go into other relationships over and over. Keep in mind that there is usually a reason why people act the way they do.

Sometimes this can also be generational. If a man saw his father do this to his mother, he believes this is the way of life. This is how life and marriage really is supposed to be.

There are times a woman will take advantage of a man's state of mind. Remember some women of today want a man whether he is married or not and some women prefer married men because they have no commitment to them.

Take a step back and see if you played a significant part in his choice of having the affair when you begin to suspect or are confronted by his choices. This means that you have found evidence of the affair. You may have found a receipt for flowers and candy, and you know that you never smelled one petal or tasted one morsel of chocolate. Maybe your phone bill went up, and you noticed a phone number that reoccurred often. You might find a receipt for a hotel that you did not enjoy yourself. You have a bill for jewelry you have never seen. Stop right here and think. You can blow up, fight, and get angry, which will probably be your first reaction. Think. Will this fight send him, in his anger, running to her for comfort? Is there something I can do to keep him at home that will bring us closer together? Are there issues that I am not handling properly? As a wife, you will have to dig sometimes into the person that you married and call your husband. Most of the time the basis for the hard truth is that when is comes down to it, the real thing is that something is lacking in the marriage.

Many times women in the world know how to fight for what they want, and what they want is your husband. But do you, as a believer, know how to strategize and fight for your marriage? The first question to ask yourself is, do I want my marriage to work? If yes, pray and ask for direction because every situation is different, and what worked for another wife may not work in your situation. Think about the result and what it is you desire to achieve. Is it to be in a wonderful relationship with your husband with love, joy, peace, and happiness? Could it be that you would like him to adore you? Would you like the pleasure of enjoying each other's company? Begin there and work in the best way you know how toward the result. What is it going to take for the both of you to get there? Keep in mind that sometimes you will be in the battle for your marriage, all by yourself for a while. Because he may not have a clue of what really needs to take place to bring the marriage into its proper state.

You can seek advice from a counselor or your pastor. Look for wise counsel. There are many friends and family members that are quick to tell you to leave your husband without knowing the circumstances. It is important to be guided by someone who will not judge him or you. Find someone that really has a heart for women and their marriages. Keep searching, seeking, and looking until you get answers. When you receive the answers, put everything on the table, study it, and then and only then make a decision.

You will go through a process of confession, repentance, or forgiveness, grieving, and making amends.

The confession comes after the knowledge of the affair has come to your attention. Here it is, now what. The person acknowledges that they had an affair. Yes, they did enter into a relationship with someone else. Here is usually when all the details are talked about—the who, what, when, where, why, and how.

The repentance is saying I am sorry. Saying I am sorry is good, but what are you sorry for? Is the person sorry for getting caught, or are they truly sorry for entering into another relationship while they are married? While you stand face-to-face, can the person say that they are sorry along with the reasons why? Truly feeling sorry deep within is not only saying I am sorry, but showing it to also be true. You stood before God to give your marriage vows, and now you must stand before God and say you are truly sorry.

Grieving—you will cry like someone died. Has your marriage died, and is it over? You may not want to get out of bed. Facing another day can bring another day of torment. You may cry while you are driving and cry yourself to sleep. You misplace things and cannot find things that are right under your nose. Your ability to reason and think shuts down. Hopelessness may sit down and stay a while. The only thing that helps is prayer and time.

Forgiveness—even though you still hurt, you find it within yourself to forgive. I mean really forgive. When you forgive, you let go of holding on to anger, resentment, and hopelessness. Forgive him and forgive yourself. You may not be able to do this immediately. It takes time and the healing of your heart.

Making amends—how do we put this behind us and start again? The affair happened, and do I really want to give up my life as a wife? Do I want to give up the marriage that I have vowed to stay in for better for worse? It did not say what the worse would be, but here we are. Keep working toward the goal of a wonderful marriage.

All of these stages will need to be worked through.

Don't keep secrets. If someone is pursuing, you tell your husband about it. Tell him what happened immediately. Set boundaries with opposite-sex friends. Stick to the limits that you have set. Intimate conversation is not to be tolerated, and be very careful. This is usually a setup. A setup that can change your life and the lives of many people around you.

If the shoe is on the other foot, and you are the one in the affair, ask yourself why, and dig deep within yourself for answers. You might be surprised at what you will discover. Ask yourself again, "Do I want my marriage?" If yes, stop the affair now. Cut it off immediately. The affair can and will not only affect you but your spouse and children to name a few. You can change their thinking about marriage forever. You can see from TV and hear in music all the affairs that go on each day. Your children see and hear and think: this is normal. Why get married. They see a lot of the incorrect ways of marriage, now let them see the correct way. The ways of marriage that is not readily shown to us every day.

Think of the result you desire in your marriage. Just as above, start there from where you are and work toward the goal. Infidelity has been going on from the beginning of time, your marriage is not the first and definitely will not be the last. But you can be one of the marriages that can survive. Remember, God forgave you for your sins, and can you forgive others as he has done for you?

Part 4

INTIMACY AND LOVE

Knowing the most private and personal parts of your husband's life is your foundation for a intimate relationship. One of our assignments as a wife is to create an atmosphere for intimacy to enter into your relationship with your husband. Intimacy is you seeing the deepest parts into him and him seeing the deepest parts of you. Your husband has places that hold the deepest darkest secrets, the places that his heart has sealed off and out of sight. There are places in him that have been concealed from the world and are invisible to the naked eye.

These secrets may have never been resolved or told to anyone. It can be secrets of abuse he suffered as a child or even as a young adult. Your husband can have issues with parents or loved ones in his family or in past friendships. There may be things that he feels about himself that he feels others would not understand, situations that are embarrassing to him or may have cause for shame to rise up in his spirit. To him, these things are important enough to keep them to himself, many times, at all cost. Nevertheless, they are his feelings. There could be incidents that occurred with complete strangers that changed his life forever. Things that could make him see life through completely different eyes. Some things he may have buried so deep within that he has forgotten all about them until something happens in your marriage and all the memories will begin to unfold right before your eyes. If and when this may occur, you must be a strong and patient wife. Be a wife that can and will have the endurance to run this race to the end.

Intimacy is an honor and a privilege. You are sharing part of his life that is not open to everyone. This is where cherished memories are created. You will have memories that are shared just between the two of you. Intimacy is where your best and your worst times are revealed. When someone cares enough about you to share their innermost feelings, they have given you something that is very precious. It is like they gave you a diamond to have and to hold. Every secret, every incident, every emotion, and every circumstance—each one is a precious diamond that he has given to you to hold. Think about this for a minute, if someone gave you a container full of diamonds, what would you do. Would you shout to the world, "I have a container full of diamonds!"? Let me tell you about them. Would you take the container around and show the diamonds to everyone that was curious about what you had? A wise woman would take the container of diamonds and put them away in a safe place. She would keep the diamonds in a vault or a safe, locked away until the time comes to bring them out again in an intimate moment.

Usually the secrets that he hold can be very emotional, and he may need to lay in your breast for comfort. He may need you to hold him and stroke him to comfort and calm his nerves.

Touch is very important. It is a sense that we use every day. There is power in touch. The benefits of touch can manifest itself in many different ways. Touch can heal. When someone is ill, touch can make them feel better. Touch can soothe the soul and can be shown in intimacy and love.

In the case of men and women, a touch can express you care. By holding hands, in this touch you can feel the softness or coarseness of the skin, its warmth, or coolness. In this touch, you will feel the texture of the skin in every finger that is caressed, either entwined or folded together. Hand holding can make statements of "I love you, I want to be with you," or "I want you to be here close to me, I am aware that you are here, you protect me, you guide me, and you care for me."

When a loved one passes on, you can see that hand holding is important. It provides comfort and shows love. Some people will kiss the hands and rub the hands tenderly. This touch is a touch you will more than likely remember the rest of your life. It is a touch that can never be replaced.

In young love or first loves, hand holding is as frequent as breathing. The couple desire to be close all the time. They are always touching, showing love to and from one another. At the first contact of holding hands, the couple instantly become aware of one another, and every sense in their bodies comes alive and is stimulated. Remember back, for the wives that have been married for a while, remember when one touch from him would make your whole body tingle with delight. The moving of a strand of hair out of your face or the hand that stroked your cheek or the way he touched any part of you skin, the arm, the foot, the leg, or shoulder.

Touch is something we think about how it feels to us (as wives), more than how we feel to someone else (to our husbands). How much do you touch your husband? He needs you to touch him, stroke his head, and run your fingers though his hair. By any chance he does not have hair, rub his bald head with tenderness. Touch his ear with your breathe, and say a loving word that can linger for days. He desires to feel you. Let's go a little deeper into what touch is all about.

In infants, touch has the effects of bringing parent and child closer together, making for a closer attachment or bonding. Touch in infants develops their deep thinking skills and stimulates their thought process. They can be friendly and will enjoy the company of others. Their ability to withstand stress becomes stronger, and they develop a strong immune system. In massage and touch therapies for infants, it has been found to enhance growth and development also reducing pain. Touch is helpful in releasing endorphins in the brain that cause a pain-relieving effect. Infants who are stroked make better eye contact. They smile more and show more vocal expression; also they spend less time crying.

If touch has this effect on infants, which are just little people, what effects could it have on your husband? Touch would bring you closer together, making a stronger bond between man and wife. His reasoning could become clearer. He could be friendlier and enjoy being around other people. He could handle stress better. He would be sick less often. You could relieve his headache, neck pain, or shoulder tightness.

At work, he will be able to make better eye contact, showing a stronger personality. That may bring about a promotion. He would smile more and talk to you more and spend less time in a bad mood. Now can you understand why your husband enjoys sex? A touch can make the difference.

HUGS

I have found that few people can be comfortable with hugs. Hugs are when you put your arms around someone and hold them closely; you squeeze them tight and embrace all that they are. There are hugs that let you know I love you and let you know that you are loved. You will find that there are hugs that are a quick squeeze and let you go. There are hugs that hold you and give you a pat on the back or shoulder. Some hugs are a full embrace. this hug has a firm tight squeeze, and they can seem to go on forever.

My pastor taught me a lot about how to hug. My first experiences with her hugs were quite unnerving. She wrapped her arms around me and held me close. Her arms were firm and steady. This type of hug was so unfamiliar to me. I would think to myself, "Okay, when she going to let me go?" Any minute now, she is going to let me go. She still held on to me with a tight embrace. I tried to back away and do a shoulder shrug that I thought would send a signal of "you can let go of me now." When she would feel you relax and surrender to the love she was giving to you, then and only then she would let you go. I began to say hello from afar. But you know, this woman would always catch me for a hug. She must have had some kind of love radar that told her I needed a big hug and some love shown to me on that day.

I learned something about myself through that experience. In this experience, I learned that I was not accustomed to hugging. I was uncomfortable with closeness, and I did not love as deeply as I could. I questioned and searched myself. My thoughts were did I hug my children enough? Did I show them love and affection and let them know that I cared and was concerned about their well-being? How did I hug my sisters, brothers, parents, and most importantly, how did I hug my husband?

My mother-in-law had hugs that would always make you smile. You would laugh and be tickled pink. She would hug you so tight and then give you as many kisses as she could that would tickle you and make you laugh out loud. I call them tickle kisses. She was a woman of small stature, only about four feet eleven inches tall. She would only be able to reach your neck, or sometimes, if you bent down far enough, she could reach your cheek. That was a hug that she passed on to me, and I give them away as much as possible. Those hugs with tickle kisses have become a part of me.

Touch your husband often. Your touch can relax him or excite him. Whatever the touch is, it can relax him and give him time to trust and open up to new thoughts, new directions, and most of all, to open up to your love.

As you can see, touch is very important to our existence. Can you imagine with me for a moment? Out there in this vast world we live in, there are people that live every day without a touch. Examine your life. How many times a day do you touch someone? Let us let love survive. Expand your experiences with life and change your lifestyle by keeping in touch with your husband.

SEX

Sex is one of the greatest concerns in the marriage relationship. Sex is also one of the major reasons people get divorced. When couples are not having sex with each other or are having sex with other people besides their spouse, there is something to be concerned about.

Sex with your husband does include intimacy and love. When you have a husband, you can be free to have any kind of sex you both agree upon. You must do your best to remove thoughts of the past when you were told that sex was nasty. Some women were told that a man's penis is dirty. Depending on what is in your past, whether it is abuse or very strong beliefs passed down from other people in authority in our lives. If you search for answers, more than not you will find out that what you thought and believed was entirely incorrect.

A man (your husband) is very visual and analytical. He takes notice of what is around him and you on a daily basis. In the media, on TV, most of the entertainment include some kind of sexual influence. To sell butter or toothpaste, they show a sexual scene that has nothing to do with what they are selling. Music will sometimes sing you the entire sexual experience. Regular magazines show naked people or have very suggestive modeling pose. Sexy is in, and there are people that feel that they want to bring sexy back.

Your husband is bombarded with sex every day. Beautiful women are everywhere and even if you believe that a woman is not beautiful. Believe me, that is not what will always get the man. Men are attracted to flesh. They can see a multitude of flesh every day. Even though he is trying to be the best husband he knows how to be, he still will have a challenge with keeping his eyes from wandering. Some women have so much flesh exposed they even make other women look. You may have to tell some women to get their you know whatever out of his face.

Give the man a break; it can be difficult for him to control those eyes. Help him by letting him know what his eyes are doing. Over time he will be able to get a bit better at controlling his eyes.

I would like to give you some information on a few things that may come up during you marriage that can hinder your sex drive as you live the life of a wife.

Your use of antidepressants can decrease sexual desire. This does not occur in everyone, but many find out, after they begin treatment, that it does affect their desire for sexual intimacy.

Your body image and how you see yourself matter too. You may see yourself as unattractive to your husband, and guess what? What you believe has a huge effect on your relationship. If you see yourself as unattractive, you will act unattractive, you will feel unattractive, and to others, you may have an unattractive look. Think positive.

If you are breast-feeding, there is a hormone called prolactin that reduces sexual interest.

The hormone is instrumental in producing breast milk. Know that this can happen, and be patient; breast-feeding does not last forever.

When you have disagreements or arguments with you husband, this can cut the desire to have sex off quickly. So make an effort to resolve conflicts as soon as possible. Making up with you husband can bring about wild and passionate sex.

Some wives have a fear of intimacy. Sex brings two people as close together as you can possible get, and some wives, for many reasons, cannot handle the closeness. They will not feel like being that close to their husbands, so the sex drive decreases. Sex may become less and less important.

A change in hormones can change you sexual desire. For women, low levels of free testosterone or high levels of sex hormone binding globulin (SHBG) can decrease your desire for sex. Hormones play a big part in a woman's life. Many women go through the continuous battle of the hormones with monthly periods, and when menopause arrives, we may go through the constant change. Sexual desire can also be decreased due to vaginal dryness that can occur during this time of your life.

No sleep or lack of sleep can cause a woman to think about sex, but she does not have the energy to act on the thoughts. Especially after you have been married for a while, sleep comes before sex any day.

Use of oral contraceptives for some women can cause loss of sexual desire. The use of any of the hormonal approaches to birth control may cause you, as a woman, side effects that can reduce your desire for sex.

Stress is a major cause that women have a decrease in sexual desire. Stress causes tension in your muscles or your muscles feel tight and hard to the touch. Stress can make you feel jumpy, irritable, or unable to concentrate. Under stress, your heart will beat at a faster rate, headaches are common, and the stiff neck and tight shoulders affect your day. You may have a backache, rapid breathing, or your palms will be sweaty; your stomach is upset, and you feel nausea and may vomit or have diarrhea. Stress can produce skin problems such as acne or psoriasis. Your immune system will become weak, and you may become sick easier. Stress can cause painful menstrual periods.

Stress can show up not only in your body, but can alter your mood and your thinking. Little things that usually do not bother you will cause you to lose your temper and yell at the people you love for no apparent reason. You may feel tired all the time and worry about things that you cannot do anything about. Negative images of yourself appear, and you will begin to doubt your abilities to get things done.

You will find that men also have reasons why they do not want to have sex with their wives. One reason could be that they are masturbating. It is easy and can be done anywhere or anytime they are stimulated throughout the day and can be done all by themselves without the closeness of intimacy. Another reason is that the husband is having sex with another partner. This has the possibility of being male or female partner.

Another is hormonal; he may have problem getting or keeping an erection. The desire to have sex may just not be there. Another reason may be that sex with you may not be fulfilling. Wives can have poor hygiene, like not bathing and keeping the genital areas clean or having constant bad breath. Your husband may be interested in other sexual activities, and the both of you have not yet come to some agreement. There may be something that you do in the sexual act that turns him off even if you do not intentionally try to do so. This could be due to some kind of abuse, so keep lines of communication open.

You can handle some of these issues by reading or searching deep within your soul or from an open communication. Professionals may need to be sought out to handle other issues. Check with your doctors about your situation, and you may need the help of a therapist. Find people to help you. They are out there, and they are there to help you. Look and you will find someone that can give you the information you need to help you in your situation.

Creativity can be a way to increase sexual activity. Create a special evening once a week or once a month or whenever you decide. Create something he will be sure to enjoy. Remember to include all of the senses.

Taste—Good food and drinks; something he would enjoy or something to taste that would be adventurous.

Smell—aromatherapy is a great way to enhance the mood. Fragrant oils or lotions can also help.

Vision—get a vision. Remember men are visual so you can really play this one up. Create a vision and you might even need the help of someone you know that is a decorator and has many creative abilities.

Hearing—beautiful sounds that inspire the mood you are going to create. Play music or have sounds of waterfalls or the sounds of the ocean waves coming to meet the shore or the sounds of the forest with birds and the rustling of the leaves on the trees. I hope that you are getting the idea.

Touch—include touch in everything you create.

Let me give you an example. Your husband comes home. On his arrival, the house smells of your great cooking. You are dressed beautifully, girly and feminine. He has a wonderful dinner, drinks, and conversation. You have placed a string on his chair that has love notes all the way to the bedroom. You have spent time preparing the bedroom. You make sure that it is a retreat from the world. This means that you do not have a computer in the room and lots of exercise equipment; remember, you are creating a retreat. So work areas gone. In your bedroom retreat, you only include things that are relaxing and inviting. On your bed, you have purchased eight-hundred-thread count sheets or higher. You can purchase these on the Internet for very good prices. So that once he hits those sheets, every thought of the day will disappear, and the sheets smell of your perfume. Take time to find the best bedding your money can buy. When he enters the bedroom, have rose petals, real or artificial, all over the room and/or on the bed in a shape of a heart and/or with a note attached, telling him what he means to you. On the side of the bed, you can have drinks and desserts like strawberries or some kind of fresh fruits. Be creative and sensitive to his likes and dislikes. Some men may prefer strawberries dipped in chocolate or maybe just chocolate. Pineapples dipped in chocolate are also a tasty treat. Have him a bath ready with all the aromatherapy to go with it. While he is in the bath, you get ready and change into something special. When his bath is over, make sure he has a warm towel to dry himself off, or you can do it for him. You can also bathe him if you like. This is an example; you know your husband, and you can be the creator of your vision. Usually by this time, he is ready to enjoy the evening. I will let you take it from here. Get a vision, be creative, and create a retreat.

LOVE

Love is an intensified feeling of caring. Love goes deeper than any of our thoughts of what love is. Many times people can feel affection for someone. These are warm and tender feelings. Affection can be emotional and is when you have a soft spot in you heart for someone. You may be sentimental over the person. Affection is not as powerful or as deep as love.

We can attach ourselves to someone. We may become connected by ties of affection. You can become attached to a beautiful set of dishes passed down in the family. Maybe your attachment is to a special piece of furniture. You can also attach yourself to people, whether they lift you up or put you down. You are attached to their presence. Attachment is not as powerful or as deep as love.

There is also an emotion of infatuation. When you are in this mode, you do not think properly. Infatuation will have you doing foolish things. Crazy things you probably said you would never do. You have developed a passion that cannot be reasoned with. Your family and friends can see that you are in an infatuated emotional rollercoaster. You may think to yourself they do not understand. You cannot see the forest because of the trees. Infatuation is temporary and does not last. Infatuation is not as powerful or as deep as love.

Many times, we as women are confused as to what love is all about, and these three—affection, attachment, and infatuation—are sometimes mistaken for love.

There are different types of love. Each type has its own level of action associated within itself.

Phileo love is also known as brotherly love. This is the love you have toward one another in mankind. The type of love you show to your friends and people you meet. It is the love of people. You can show consideration for others, caring for them as you would care for yourself.

Phileo is where you begin to develop relationships. Building the foundations for friendships is important. I give you a place to start knowing love. In this place is where a husband and wife should start their journey into love. In some marriages, this is a missing link. Husbands and wives forget that your spouse is your best friend. Knowing what is in the heart of the other person, your husband needs for you to be a friend, a friend that he can share much laughter and joy with. Sharing the days and nights of his life, no matter how exciting or insignificant they may seem. Through the ups and the downs, he can look to the side and see that you are still there. When no one else is there, he can count on his wife to be there. If there is someone that he needs to call, it would be you. Building a relationship together takes time and communication. People do change over the years. His favorite color may change, the way he cuts his hair may change. So get to know who he is today. Every day is another day into the journey of getting to know true love. Friendships turn into deeper love. Go deeper into a friendship with your husband. Call him as much as possible just to say hello. Purchase cards or small tokens of appreciation and write him letters. Pick up some beautiful stationary and spray it with your fragrance. Let him know that you care. It is what friends do.

Eros love is sexual love. It is where we get the word erotic. Eros love is sex with love. We know that it is possible to have sex without love. Sex without love is sex in lust, which only cares about itself. Lust wants to feel good, it wants to unleash what is inside of itself. Lust wants to feel better about itself, but what lust really desires is to feel love. This emotion cannot feel love even though it is what it desires most. Again and again, it tries to fulfill itself, but lust does not last and cannot fill the soul. It does not have love or feel love, but the craving of love can move lust into disastrous behaviors.

Eros love is the love between a husband and a wife that includes sex. There is good sex and better sex, but the best is when you have sex that is completely in love. This type of love says, "You are the one that I want. You are the one that I am committed to." This kind of love creates new life.

Sexual love brings a husband and wife closer together. It creates intimacy between the two of them like no other in the world. The man into the woman is forming a bond or a soul tie to one another. The couple cares for each other and cares about each other, sharing the love that each of them hold and so want to freely give.

Agape love is unconditional love. It is love that is given to us from God and the love that comes from us to God. I find that 1 John 4:7-21 (amplified version) explains the love of God.

Beloved, let us love one another, for love is (springs) from God; and he who loves [his fellowmen] is begotten (born) of God and is coming [progressively] to know and understand God [to perceive and recognize and get a better and clearer knowledge of Him]. He who does not love has not become acquainted with God [does not and never did know Him], for God is love. In this the love of God was made manifest (displayed) where we are concerned: in that God sent His Son, the only begotten [Son], into the world so that we might live through Him. In this is love: not that we loved God, but that He loved us and sent His Son to be the propitiation (the atoning sacrifice) for our sins. Beloved, if God loved us so [very much], we also ought to love one another. No man has at any time [yet] seen God. But if we love one another, God abides (lives and remains) in us and His love (that love which is essentially His) is brought to completion (to its full maturity, runs its full course, is perfected) in us! By this we come to know (perceive, recognize, and understand) that we abide (live and remain) in Him and He in us: because He has given (imparted) to us of His [Holy] Spirit. And [besides] we ourselves have seen (have deliberately and steadfastly completed) and bear witness that the Father has sent the Son [as the] Savior of the world. Anyone who confesses (acknowledges, owns) that Jesus is the Son of God, God abides (lives, makes His home) in him and the [abides, lives, makes his home] in God. And we know (understand, recognize, are conscious of, by observation and be experience) and believe (adhere to and put faith in and rely on) the love God cherishes for us. God is love, and he who dwells and continues in love dwells and continues in God, and God dwells and continues in him. In this [union and communion with Him] love is brought to completion and attains perfection with us, that we may have confidence for the Day of Judgment [with assurance and boldness to face Him], because as he is so are we in this world. There is no fear in love [dread does not exist], but full-grown (complete, perfect) love turns fear out of doors and expels every trace of terror! For fear brings with is the thought of punishment, and [so] he who is afraid has not reached the full maturity of love [is not yet grown into love's complete perfection]. We love Him, because He first loved us. If anyone says, I love God, and hates (detests, abominates) his brother [in Christ], he is a liar; for he who does not love his brother, whom he has seen, cannot love God, Whom he has not seen. And this command (charge, order, and injunction) we have from Him: that he who loves God shall love his brother [believer] also.

God's love is unconditional. It is a divine love given freely to us. Whether you accept it or not, or you see it, experience it, or feel it, God's love is always there. It is yours for asking. When you ask, believe, and you will receive. Love God with all your heart, with all your soul, and with all your strength.

Once you have experienced this type of love you will come to know and understand much more of what true love is all about. This love will truly change your life. When you walk with love and talk with love, your entire being changes, and you will begin to live through your circumstances differently. Your life will begin again on a foundation of love. You can build better relationships with others and build a better relationship with yourself.

Anything done in love makes a difference. For instance, when a meal is prepared with love, you can taste the difference. When a dinner party is prepared with love, you can see and feel the difference. Love added to anything heightens the experience.

Take a piece of paper; make a line in the middle of the page from top to bottom. On the left side list all the things you love about your husband. From the small things, like you love his smile, to larger things, like he keeps his closet neat. Write everything you can think of—all the things he does around the home, all the things he does when you entertain, all the things he does in the car or while driving. Write, write, and write.

On the right side write all the things you feel he needs to improve. Example, he does not show enough affection, again list everything you can possibly think of. Now fold the paper down the middle and from top to bottom. Look at the needs-improvement list.

On another piece of paper write your number 1 concern. Underneath it you write the opposite and/or what he needs and then write how you can help. Example, your first concern on the list is he is not affectionate enough. The opposite of this is to show lots of affection or maybe to have lots of affection.

As a helpmate (the wife), how can you show him ways or teach him ways to be more affectionate? List anything that comes to your mind. It is now time to put what you wrote into action. For instance, after he has come home to relax, had something to eat and drink (or maybe a sexual love encounter), after his release and he is open, you can, (with love), talk to him about affection. Tell him about the things you like (some things maybe on your love list), and ask what are some of the things he enjoys. Show him some affectionate ways that please you most, like the stroking of your skin or hugs that seem to last forever. Tell him, show him, and thank him. Be grateful for even the small things.

Do your best at recognizing when he needs a sexual release. He needs your love. This is a time of trust and a very private, intimate moment in a marriage. There may be times when he desires to tell you some of his sexual challenges. Be ready to listen. Think before you answer him. This is something he shares with no one else. Do not judge your husband. Bringing shame to him will lock his feelings away, maybe forever. He may never open up and talk with you again. Sharing with you will become null and void. If you do not know how to respond, be quiet and listen. Hold him in silence, think for a few days, and try not to treat him differently. He has exposed sexual needs, desires, his sexual thoughts and/or sexual acts. These can be things you could not have ever thought about or dreamed in your wildest dreams, but these are his thoughts and challenges. Look deeper as to what in his past might have caused these issues. Identify his strengths and weaknesses. You might suggest professional help. Love him for who he is. Help him as much as you possibly can to move forward into his destiny. Look over your love list, keep the left side close to you. Remember all the things you love about him. Read your love list, tell him the things you love about him, and most of all, show what you love in your actions.

CONCLUSION

Living the life of a wife can be the most challenging experience of a lifetime. If you really love your husband, and your desire is to keep you marriage together, make a decision to try everything you possibly know. And when you have tried ten out of ten things, try number eleven. Do everything within your power, do everything you know how to do before you call your marriage over. Pray to God for answers. Ask God for direction. Listen and look for the answers he sends to you. Sometimes the answer comes though the craziest vessels. But listen and think, then pray and think some more. I have seen alcoholics become the king of the castle and the priest of their homes, treating their wives as the queen she is. Husbands that are drug addicts change their lives and become the best of the best husbands. Liars and cheaters become the most true and faithful husbands. If you feel deep within your heart, and you can see some glimmer of hope, fight for your marriage.

Many things come to separate a husband and wife. Your marriage can survive. There are different seasons or times in a marriage. Ecclesiastes 3:1-8 reads

To everything, there is a season. A time for every purpose under heaven. A time to be born, and a time to die. A time to plant, and a time to pluck what is planted. A time to kill, and a time to heal. A time to break down, and a time to build up. A time to weep, and a time to laugh. A time to mourn, and a time to dance. A time to cast away stones, and a time to gather stones. A time to embrace, and a time to refrain from embracing. A time to gain, and a time to lose. A time to keep, and a time to throw away. A time to tear, and a time to sew. A time to keep silence, and a time to speak. A time to love, and a time to hate. A time of war, and a time of peace.

Know that you will go through many of these times. Be patient times, are always changing. There are circumstances where you might have to walk away or you may have been the one that stayed as he walked away from you. Hold on, there are others like yourself; find the ones that have wisdom, and find comfort in what they have to give you. Even though you feel you will lose your mind, you will survive, there are other men out there looking for a good wife. When you have come back to yourself, continue to work on you.

Look into the mirror and stick out your tongue. I challenge you to stop your tongue from moving. Hold your tongue with your fingers if you must. Stop all movement of your tongue. Put your all into it. Just stop it.

You cannot stop the tongue from moving. Have you ever seen a power line break and the power causes the line to spark and move and wiggle all over the place? It may fly into the air or have wild movements over the ground. The Bible says in Proverbs 18:21, Death and life are in the power of the tongue. There is power in your tongue. That is why you cannot stop it from moving; like that power line, there is power within your tongue. The tongue has power you have not used yet. You have the power to speak those things as you have thought them. You have the power to change the atmosphere around you with your tongue. Your tongue says things that your ears can hear and your heart can receive. Speak life with your tongue. Talk about the things you desire. Talk to yourself about how wonderful you are, how beautiful you are. Talk about the type of marriage you want. Every time you open your mouth, let words come out that will encourage, comfort, and inspire someone else and yourself. You have got to act now with what you have learned. Use the power you have been given, and continue to live the best life of a wife you can possibly know.

Part 5

A Wife's Prayer

Father God,

You are the creator of all things, and there is nothing that was created without you. You are a wondrous and loving God, awesome in all your ways. Thank you for being my God. Thank you for loving me for who I am. Thank you, God, because it is only by your grace that I am what I am. I ask that your will be continuous in my life, Father. I pray today, Father, for your help. Help me. I need you to come into me and into my life. I desire, Father God, to know you and your ways. Teach me. Teach me to be the best wife to my husband that I can possibly be. Help me to speak words of encouragement, words that will inspire, comfort and nurture his soul. Send your godly wisdom, knowledge, and understanding to my heart and mind. Help me to overcome the things in my past that cause me not to see your ways clearly. I am sorry, God, for not living by your word. I am sorry for the ways I have treated my husband in the past. Forgive me for all the things that I have done that are contrary to your word. Forgive me for my thoughts and actions. Bring my relationship closer to you and my husband. Draw us closer to you. I ask that all the descendents from both of our bodies will be dedicated to you; I pray that they will serve you and forever praise the name of the Lord. Cover my family under the wings of your glory. Protect us and guide us through this life. Keep my husband and myself from the temptations of this world. Direct our footsteps, God. Continue to consume our lives. I have hurt for so long, God, that I need your love to free me. Show me how to love. Let me know how to give love and to receive love. Thank you for all that you are doing and for all the things that I will recognize as you working on my behalf. I will give you all the glory and the honor, in your son Jesus' name I pray. Thank you. Amen

Here is a poem written by a very loving and dynamic woman. The poem helped me to see the beauty in the world, the beauty in a rose and most of all the beauty that is myself. I have hopes that this poem will help you as it has helped me.

The Beauty of a Rose

The Rose
The rose represents the beauty of a woman,
The stem represents her strength,
The leaves represent her forever stretched out arms,
The pedals are delicate, soft and silky like the texture of her skin,
The sweet smelling fragrance gives off an aroma that reflects her sweet disposition,
The form and shape of the rose reminds you of how God patiently took the time to
Create such an elegant piece of work,
Remember the next time you reach to pick or smell a rose
Know that the beauty of a Rose is you.

The Beauty of a Rose is _____
                          Insert your name

Index